I wish I were...

a fairy

Ivan Bulloch & Diane James

TWO-CAN™

PRINCETON ■ LONDON

www.two-canpublishing.com

Published in the United States and Canada by
Two-Can Publishing LLC
234 Nassau Street
Princeton, NJ 08542

© 2001, 1999 Two-Can Publishing

For information on Two-Can books and multimedia,
call 1-609-921-6700, fax 1-609-921-3349, or visit our website at
http://www.two-canpublishing.com

Art Director Ivan Bulloch
Editor Diane James
Illustrator Dom Mansell
Photographer Daniel Pangbourne
Models Hollie, Maryam, Eleanor, Kerry, Jasmin, Zoe,
Cory, Abigail, Courtney, Ben

HC ISBN 1-58728-036-1
SC ISBN 1-58728-040-X

HC 2 3 4 5 6 7 8 9 10 04 03 02 01
SC 2 3 4 5 6 7 8 9 10 04 03 02 01

Printed in Spain by Graficromo S.A.

Contents

If you are very, very quiet and you look very, very carefully, some people say you might one day see a fairy! Fairies are said to like to be outdoors, anywhere where there are trees, plants, and flowers, though sometimes they may come inside. Perhaps you would like to find out more about fairies? *Yes! Let's go to fairyland...*

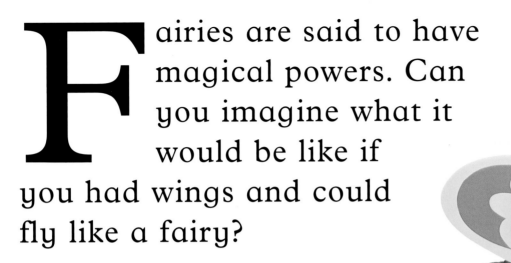

Fairies are said to have magical powers. Can you imagine what it would be like if you had wings and could fly like a fairy?

Swift, nimble, and light on their feet, fairies flutter from place to place, just like beautiful butterflies.

3 Glue the rectangle between the two wings, leaving a gap of about 2 1/2 in. (6 cm). Ask a grown-up to help you adjust the lengths of elastic to fit under your arms and around your shoulders. Tie the ends of the lengths of elastic together.

1 Cut two wing shapes like the one above from cardboard. Decorate both sides of the wings by gluing on shapes cut from colored paper. Think about butterfly wings!

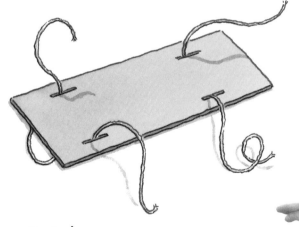

2 Ask a grown-up to cut a cardboard rectangle to fit between the wings. Make two slits on either side. Thread two lengths of elastic through the slits to go around your arms.

Fairies love pretty clothes, in all the colors of the rainbow. Sometimes they persuade a friendly spider to spin cloth as light as air. Fairies decorate their clothes and hair with freshly picked flowers.

1 Cut a rectangle about 30 in. x 20 in. (80 cm x 50 cm) of see-through material. Fold it in half and make a slit along the fold big enough to put your head through. Wear a leotard underneath.

There are lots of occasions to dress up–birthdays, new spell parties, and *especially* when the King and Queen pay a visit.

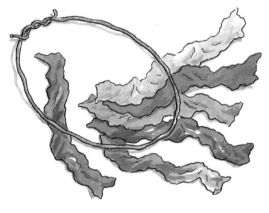

2 Now make a headdress. Ask a grown-up to cut a length of coated wire, long enough to fit around your head, and bend it into a circle. Cut wide strips of tissue paper for flowers.

3 Wind a length of tissue paper around and around in a coil and scrunch it up at one end. Tie the scrunched-up end tightly with a piece of yarn or thin ribbon. Make about 12 flowers like this.

4 Tie each flower onto the circle of wire with the yarn or ribbon. Make a knot or a bow. Keep the flowers bunched up close together.

Look, just the flower for me!

Legends say that fairies have magical powers, but they always keep their spells secret. It seems that a fairy needs a magic wand to help with the spells. Wands are passed from parents to children, and the magic never wears off! Fairies nearly always use their magic kindly, but mischievous fairies may use it to play tricks.

1 Cut a star shape, like the one in the picture, from a piece of poster board.

2 Spread some glue over one side of the star shape. Sprinkle glitter over the glue. Gently tap the star over a bowl to collect any glitter that hasn't stuck on.

Make a wish and it may come true!

3 Paint a length of dowel gold. When the paint is dry, decorate the dowel by winding some colored tape around and around in a spiral.

4 Attach the dowel to the back of the star with some wide tape. Does your wand work? Maybe you need to practice.

There are lots of different kinds of fairies–elves, brownies, goblins, leprechauns, and pixies. Some live in underground caves, some deep in the woods, others near rivers and streams. They are all extremely difficult to spot!

1 Cut a circle from a 12-in. (30-cm) square of poster board. It doesn't have to be a perfect circle, because leaves will hide the edge.

Pixies are woodland creatures. Their clothes are usually green, and they are known for their big, pointy ears!

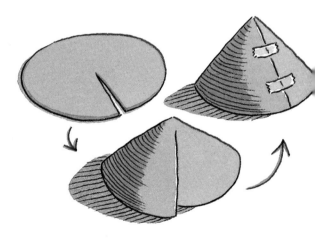

2 Cut a straight line from the outside of the circle to the middle. Gently fold one cut edge over the other to make a cone. Tape the edges in place.

3 Glue a sheet of green paper and a sheet of white paper together. With the white paper on top, tear out lots of leaf shapes.

Let's play tag in the woods. Follow me!

5 If you've got an old T-shirt, cut pointy leaf shapes at the bottom, neck, and sleeves to make an instant pixie top.

4 Start at the bottom edge of the cone and glue down a row of leaves. Overlap them slightly as you go. Keep gluing down rows of leaves, working your way up to the top of the cone. Put on your pixie hat!

Here is another character from fairyland. Gnomes are small and usually have extremely long beards. They have a very important job to do—guarding fairy treasure troves full of precious metals and wonderful jewels. They are wise and friendly, but you will hardly ever find a gnome above ground.

Do you think you would like to live underground like a gnome?

1 Cut a sheet of paper about 16 in. x 12 in. (42 cm x 30 cm). Ask a grown-up to help you shape it for your face. Leave space for your nose and a hole for your mouth.

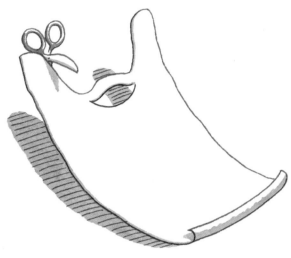

2 Starting at the opposite short end, cut slits to about half the length of the paper.

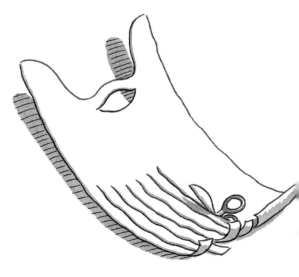

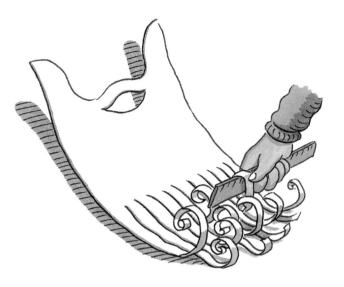

3 Gently pull one strip at a time between your thumb and a ruler. This will make the ends curl up.

4 Make a hole on either side at the top of the beard. Poke each end of a length of elastic through each hole. Knot the ends to keep them from slipping through. Slip the beard over your head and guard the jewels!

Fairies may reward human beings with a gift if they have been kind to them. This might be some money, or some fluffy fairy cakes that melt in your mouth. In return, you may want to leave a present for a fairy—maybe a glass of milk!

1 Gather together these ingredients: 4 tablespoons (50 g) margarine, 1/4 cup (50 g) sugar, 1 egg, and 1/4 cup (50 g) self-rising flour. Ask a grown-up to turn the oven to 375 °F.

2 Mix the margarine and sugar in a bowl until the mixture is pale in color. Crack the egg into the bowl and add 1 tablespoon of the flour. Beat the mixture well. Stir in the rest of the flour.

HELP YOURSELF FAIRIES!

3 Spoon equal amounts of the mixture into nine paper muffin cups on a baking sheet. The mixture should fill each cup about half way. Ask a grown-up to put them in the oven.

4 After about 20 minutes your fairy cakes should have risen—as if by magic—and changed to a golden color. Let them cool, sprinkle with tiny candies, and give someone a treat.

Let me add my spell!

Fairies keep themselves busy! As well as day-to-day tasks, they often have to prepare for special events, especially when the King and Queen are planning a visit!

Not a speck of dust in sight!

There are toadstools to dust and garlands to make. Everything must be perfect.

1 Draw a toadstool shape and a grass shape, like the ones below, on a large sheet of cardboard. Ask a grown-up to help you cut the shapes out and make slits as shown.

2 Paint the top of the toadstool red with white spots and the grass green. Paint the grass shape the same green. Slot the two shapes together.

3 Make lots of different colored tissue paper flowers like the ones on page 9. To make them into a garland, tie the flowers to a long length of colored cord or thick ribbon.

Nearly finished! Just one more flower to go!

The most important people in fairyland are the King and Queen. They spend a great deal of time traveling around fairyland making sure that all the fairies, pixies, elves, and gnomes are behaving themselves and not getting into too much mischief.

Wherever the King and Queen go there is sure to be a party, and that means everyone dresses up!

1 Make your own crown so you can be King or Queen of the Fairies. First, measure your head using a length of string. Cut a wide strip of cardboard, slightly longer than the piece of string. Glue the ends of the cardboard together.

2 Cut flower and leaf shapes from pieces of colored paper.

20

3 Glue the flower and leaf shapes onto the strip of cardboard. Overlap them as you go so that they cover the base. Put the crown on your head!

Come and join our fairy ring!

A nd so the dancing begins! The fairies skip around and around in a circle called a fairy ring. The King and Queen join in and dance the night away. Of course, there is a feast to give everyone the chance to rest before the dancing starts again. Do you think you have got enough energy to be a fairy? Why not try!

A fairy, whose life is fun and free,

Is something you may,

Or may not, ever see!

23

Fairies sometimes use words that might sound very strange to the rest of us! Here are just a few to help you carry on a fairy conversation. The words you would probably use are underneath!